MARLA FRAZEE

ROLLER COASTER

HARCOURT, INC.

San Diego   New York   London

For life's ups and downs, twists and turns...hang on tight.

Copyright © 2003 by Marla Frazee

Library of Congress Cataloging-in-Publication Data
Frazee, Marla.
Roller coaster/Marla Frazee.
p.   cm.
Summary: Twelve people set aside their fears and ride a roller coaster, including one who has never done so before.
[1. Roller coasters—Fiction.]   I. Title. PZ7.F866Ro   2003 [Fic]—dc21   2002007805
ISBN 0-15-204554-6

First edition
H G F E D C B A
Manufactured in China

The illustrations in this book were done in graphite and watercolor on Strathmore 2-ply hot press paper.
The display type was designed by Tom Seibert and rendered by Marla Frazee.

Thanks to Graham, Reed, and James, whose endless talk of roller coasters gave me the idea; Allyn Johnston, for her unflagging enthusiasm and guidance; Orrin Shively, for his roller-coaster expertise; and Leonore Cash, who made the ride less scary.

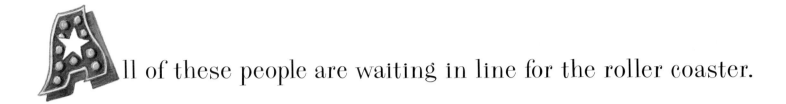

All of these people are waiting in line for the roller coaster.

Most of them have ridden on lots of roller coasters.
Some of them have only ridden on a roller coaster once or twice.

At least one of them has never ridden on a roller coaster before,

ever.

The roller coaster is very big and very noisy.

You must be tall enough to ride it.
But sometimes even those who are tall enough
decide they don't want to.
(Lots of people change their mind about riding the roller coaster
at the very last minute.)

Finally, it is time to get into the cars.

The ride operator says, "Load 'em up! Two to a seat!"

When everyone is buckled in, the operator rings a bell,
and then he releases the brake.
The train jerks forward on the tracks.
(Now it is too late for anyone to change their mind.)

S-l-o-w-l-y the train is pulled up the hill by a chain.
Clickity, clackity. Clickity, clackity. Up. Up. Up.
And then . . .

WHOOSH!

Most people scream.
Some people can't
make a sound.
And one person
can't even
open her eyes.

THE TRAIN ZIPS.

IT ZOOMS.

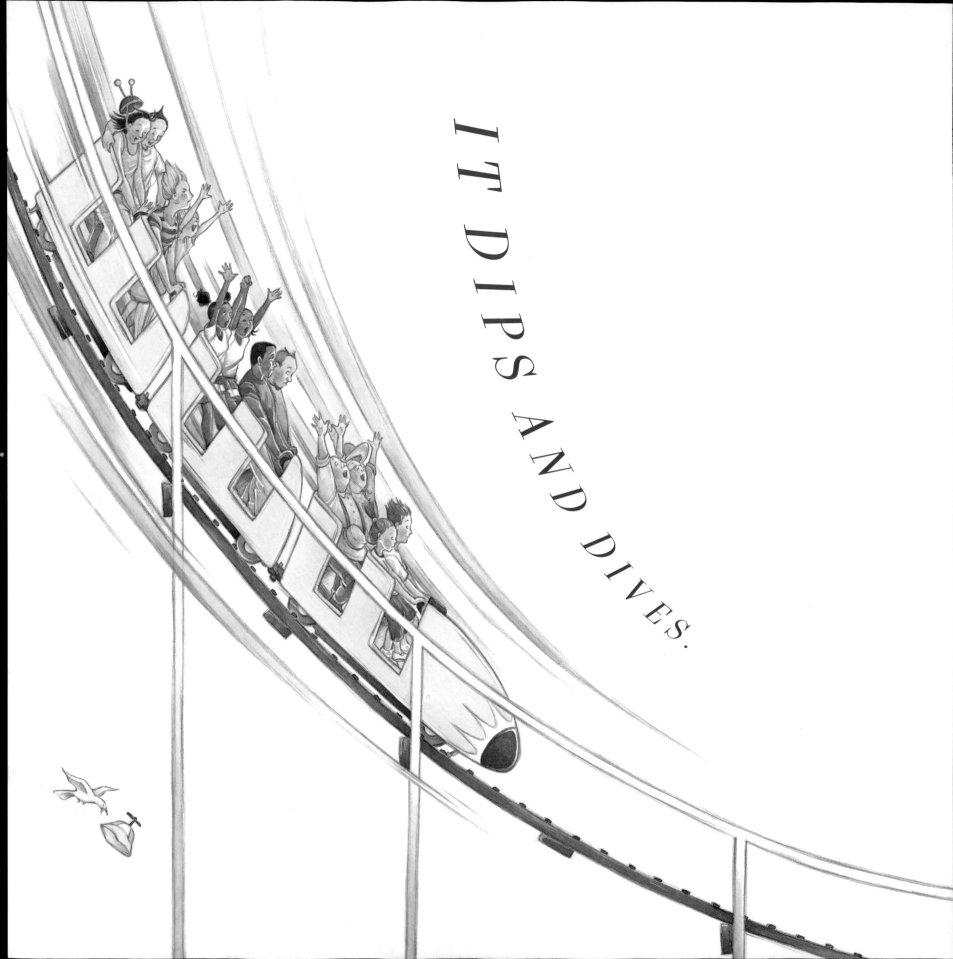

IT DIPS AND DIVES.

L-L-L THE WAY AROUND.

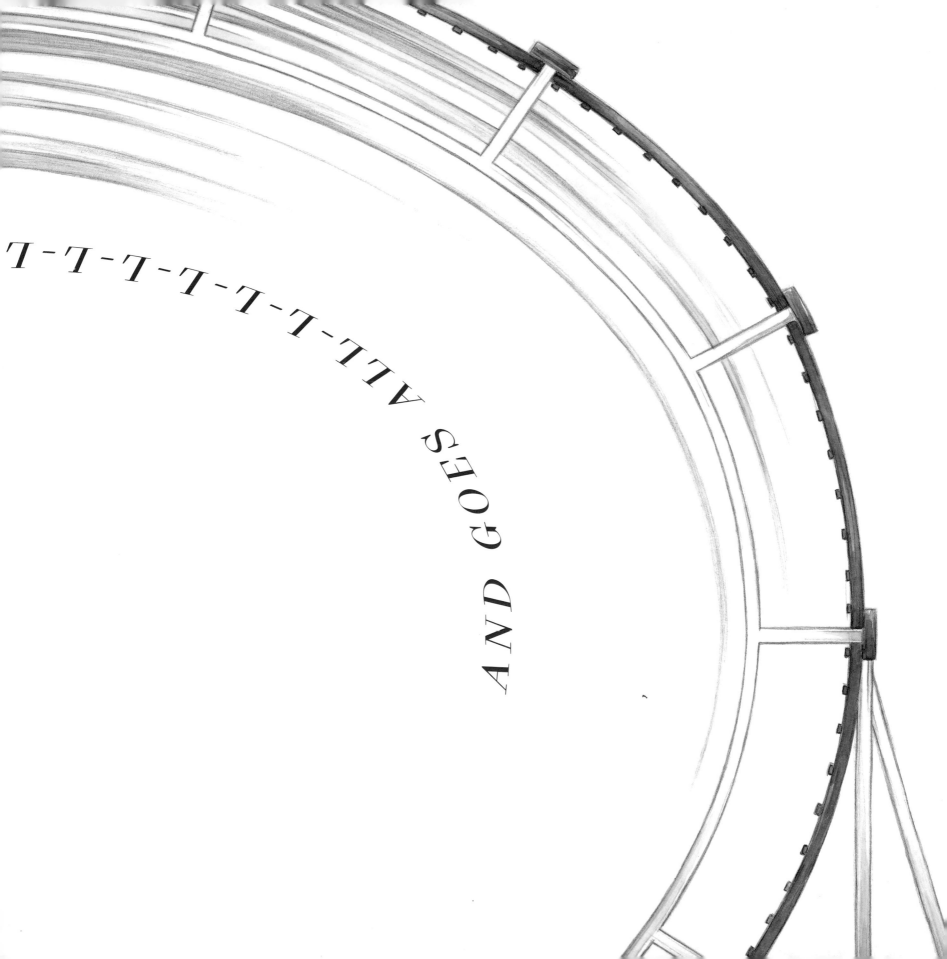

AND GOES ALL-L-L-L-L-L-L

WHEEEEEEEEEEEEEEE!

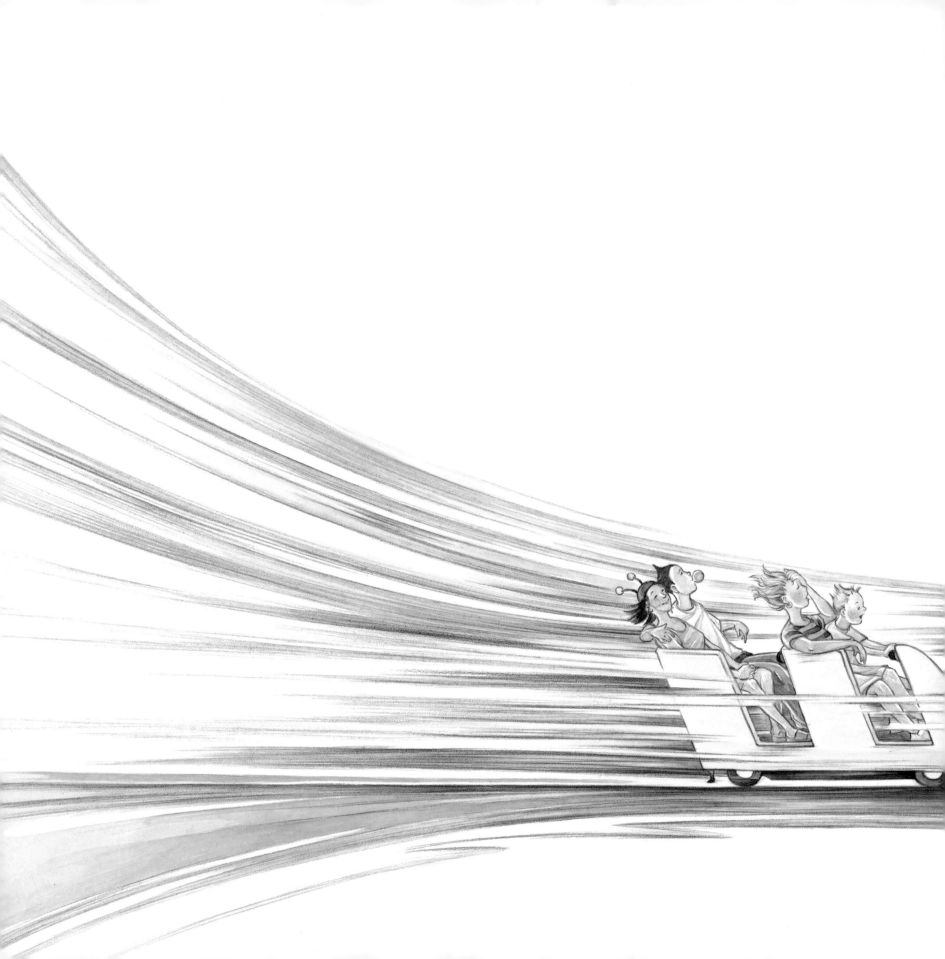

Now the ride is over.

Most of these people are dizzy.
Some of them have wobbly knees.
But at least one of them is planning
to ride the roller coaster again . . .

right now!